Christopher.

DICK KING-SMITH

Jungle Jingles

and other Animal Poems

Illustrated by Jonathan Allen

KT-574-850

JUNGLE JINGLES AND OTHER ANIMAL POEMS
A YOUNG CORGI BOOK 0552 548359

First published in Great Britain by Doubleday,
an imprint of Random House Children's Books

Doubleday edition published 1990
Picture Corgi edition published 1992
Young Corgi edition published 2002

1 3 5 7 9 10 8 6 4 2

Copyright © Fox Busters Ltd, 1990
Illustrations copyright © Jonathan Allen, 2002

The right of Dick King-Smith to be identified as the author of this work has been asserted in accordance with the Copyright, Designs and Patents Act 1988

All rights reserved. No part of this publication may be reproduced, stored in a retrieval system, or transmitted in any form or by any means, electronic, mechanical, photocopying, recording or otherwise, without the prior permission of the publishers.

Papers used by Random House Children's Books are natural, recyclable products made from wood grown in sustainable forests. The manufacturing processes conform to the environmental regulations of the country of origin.

Set in 15/20 pt Bembo Schoolbook

Young Corgi Books are published by Random House Children's Books,
61-63 Uxbridge Road, London W5 5SA,
a division of The Random House Group Ltd,
in Australia by Random House Australia (Pty) Ltd,
20 Alfred Street, Milsons Point, Sydney, NSW 2061, Australia,
in New Zealand by Random House New Zealand Ltd,
18 Poland Road, Glenfield, Auckland 10, New Zealand,
and in South Africa by Random House (Pty) Ltd,
Endulini, 5A Jubilee Road, Parktown 2193, South Africa

THE RANDOM HOUSE GROUP Limited Reg. No. 954009

A CIP catalogue record for this book is available from the British Library.

Printed and bound in Great Britain by
Cox & Wyman Ltd, Reading, Berkshire

Contents

Jungle Jingles 6
?! 8
No Wings, No Tail, Two Names 9
In the Soup 10
Tit for Tat 12
Strippers 13
Look Back in Wonder 14
Enough to Make You Sick 16
Splat! 18
Lost for Words 20
Suck it and See 22
His and Hers 23
Take Cover 24
We Have Lift-Off 26

Best Foot Forward 28
Catcall 30
Seaside Suicide 32
Like It or Lump It 34
A Family Picnic 36
Tale of a Tail 38
Fore and Aft 40
Horse Sense 41
Free Ride 42
Hear! Hear! 44
Phew! 46
Fishing Finger 48
A Game of Squash 50
Gulp! 51
Starting from Scratch 52
Jolly Blue Giant 54
Down the Hatch 56

Jungle Jingles

and other Animal Poems

www.**books**at**transworld**.co.uk/childrens

Jungle Jingles

The jungle is a fearful place
To members of the human race
Who happen to be passing through
And are not sure of what to do
In jungles, and with baited breath
Are full of thoughts of sudden death
Beneath the paws and jaws and claws
Of terrifying carnivores.

Fear not. The jungle, you should know,
Can be a thrilling place to go.
Provided that you do not sin
Against the beasts that live therein.
Shoot them with camera, not gun,
Respect them, each and every one,
And never take them unawares –
The jungle isn't yours, it's theirs.

However, should you find some day –
In spite of everything I say –
That jungles fill you with alarm,
A useful way of staying calm
And keeping cool and passing time
Is to recite a little rhyme,
You'll find your fear will soon have gone.
So here are one or two. Read on.

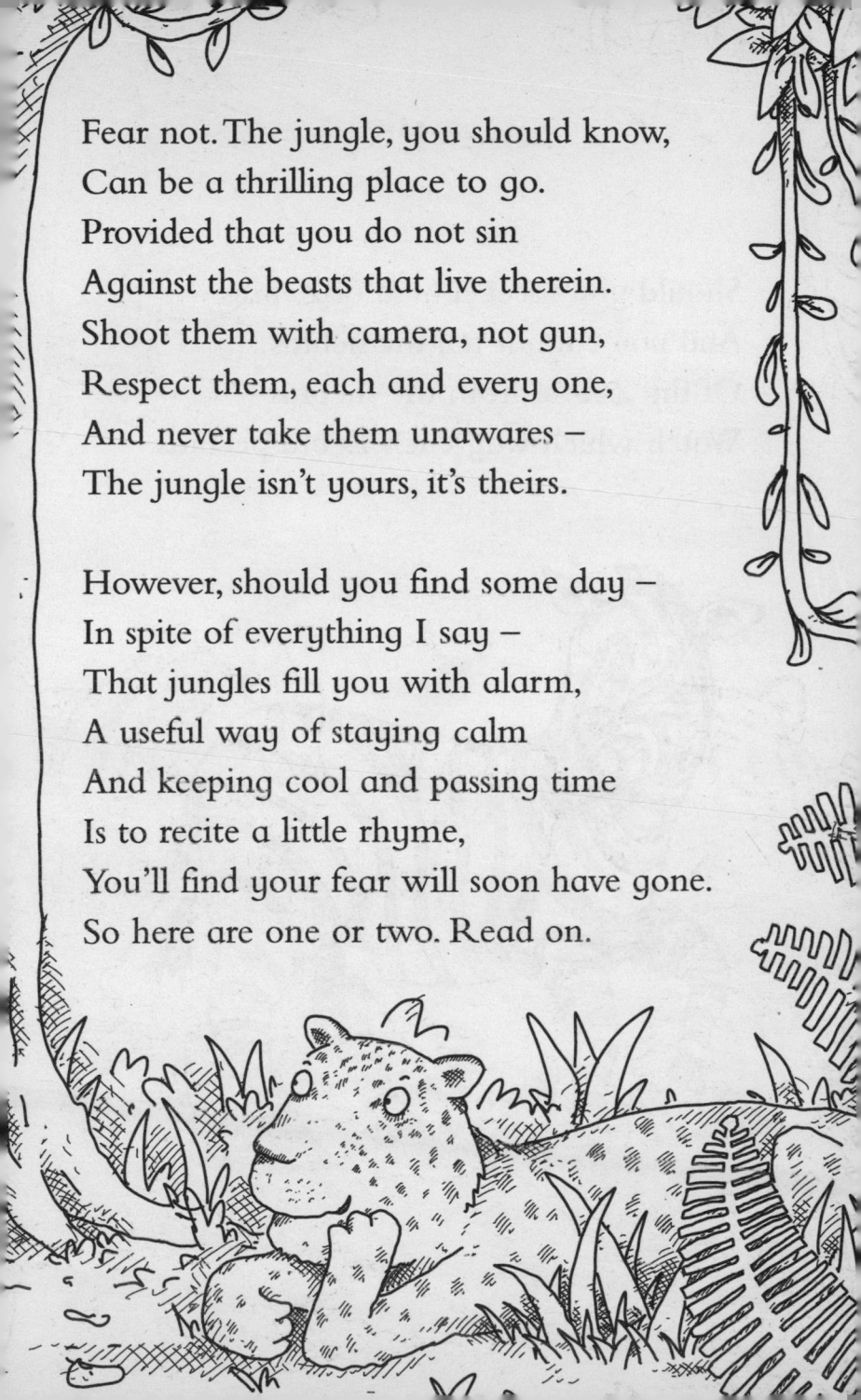

?!

Should you meet a herd of Zebras
And you cannot tell the hebras
Of the Zebras from the shebras –
Watch which way each Zebra peebras.

No Wings, No Tail, Two Names

The Kiwi's a bird with another
appellation –
The Apteryx. And, should you ever chance
to mention
This spellbinding fact to a friend or
a relation,
It's apteryxcite their immediate attention.

In the Soup

A wagging tail will tell you that
A Dog is overjoyed;
In contradiction to a Cat,
Which wags when it's annoyed.

The Ox's tail, one has to state,
Seems mournfully to droop:
It's just as though it knew its fate –
To end as oxtail soup.

Tit for Tat

The Anteater has always fed
On Ants, but when at last he's dead,
The Ants will feed on him instead.

Strippers

If you fall in a river that's full of Piranha,
They'll strip off your flesh like you'd skin
a banana.
There's no time for screaming, there's no
time for groans.
In forty-five seconds you're nothing but
bones.

Look Back in Wonder

Though the Elephant's behind
Is delightfully designed,
And the rump of any Rhino's mighty fine,
Though the buttocks of a Bear
Are indubitably fair,
And the Pig is fundamentally divine,
Though the bum of any Bison
Is a singularly nice un,
And the backside of a Boa never stops –
Yet not one's got such a bottom as
The hugeous Hippopotamus.
For bottoms, Hippopotami are tops.

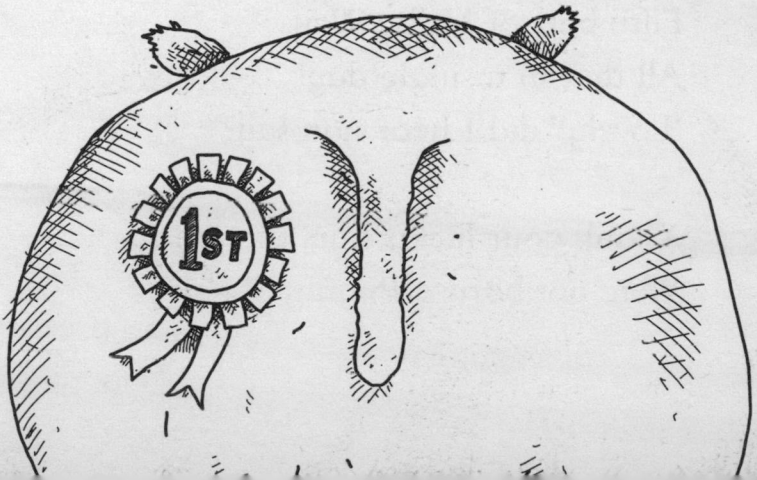

Enough to Make You Sick

What if every day you ate
Food of twice your body-weight?
That is what the Pygmy Shrew
(Just to stay alive) must do.
Think what it would mean to you.

Seven bucketfuls of chips,
Several dozen Instant Whips,
Twenty packs of Shredded Wheat,
Thirty tins of luncheon meat –
That is what you'd have to eat.

Plus – six chickens, and a ham,
Forty-seven pots of jam,
Fifty bars of Milky Way.
All that in a single day!
'Lovely!' did I hear you say?

Thank your lucky stars that you
Were not born a Pygmy Shrew.

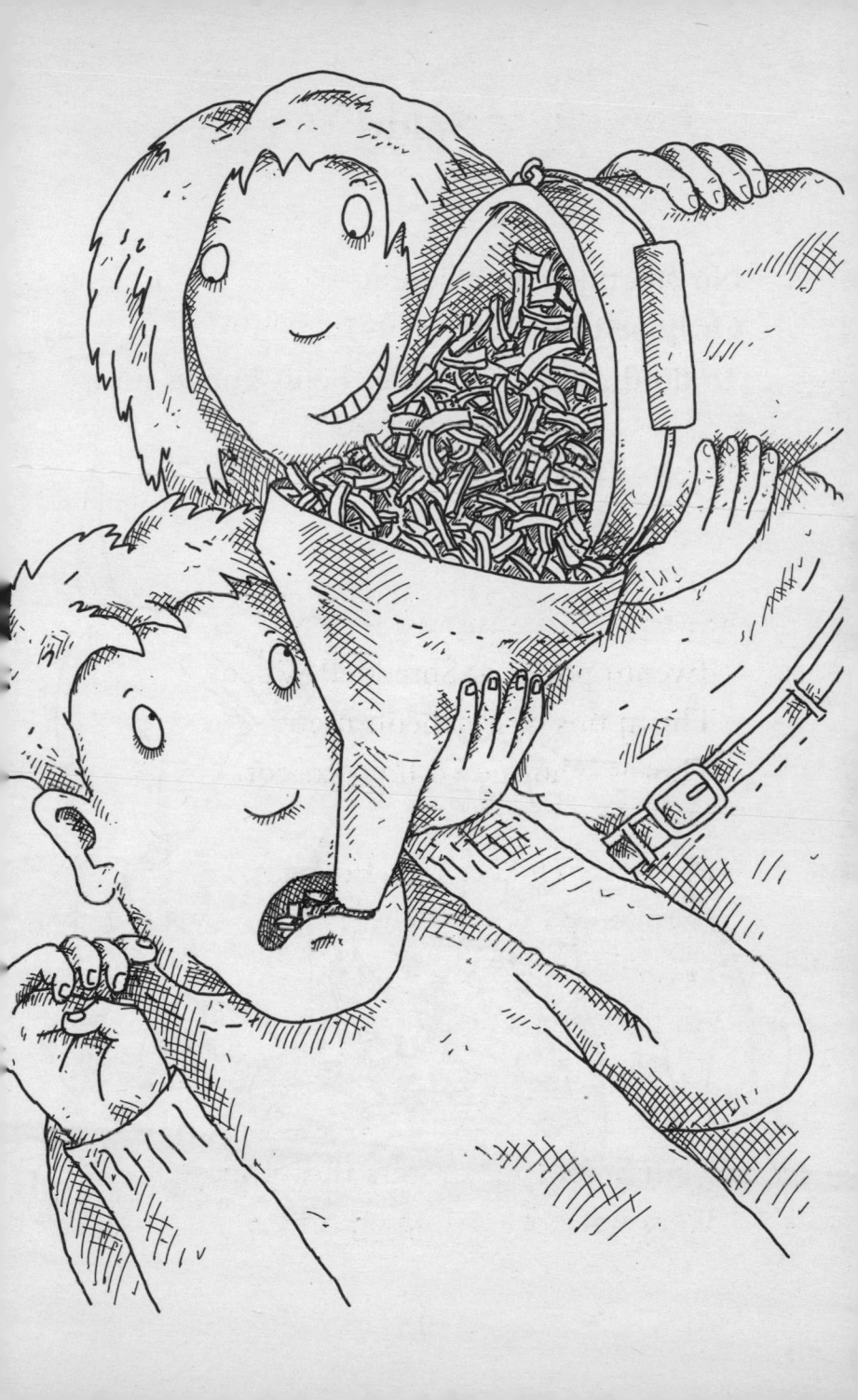

Splat!

No creature can create it
Or hope to imitate it.
To do this thing no other beast knows how.

However much they practise,
The plain and simple fact is –
No-one can make a cowpat like a Cow.

Lost for Words

A little whistling note to call its calf.
That is the only noise the tall Giraffe
Can make. Apart from that, it has no choice
But silence, for it doesn't have a voice.
For joy the tall Giraffe can never shout –
Its mouth will open, but no sound comes out.
And if it's sad or wounded or bereaved,
What happens must be seen to be believed,
For silently, out of each liquid eye,
The tears come dropping from the very sky.
Be kindly then, and never never laugh
At that dumb animal, the tall Giraffe.

Suck it and See

The taste of blood, observers note,
Is most appealing to the Stoat,
Which grabs a rabbit by the throat,
And dines upon it, table-d'hôte.

His and Hers

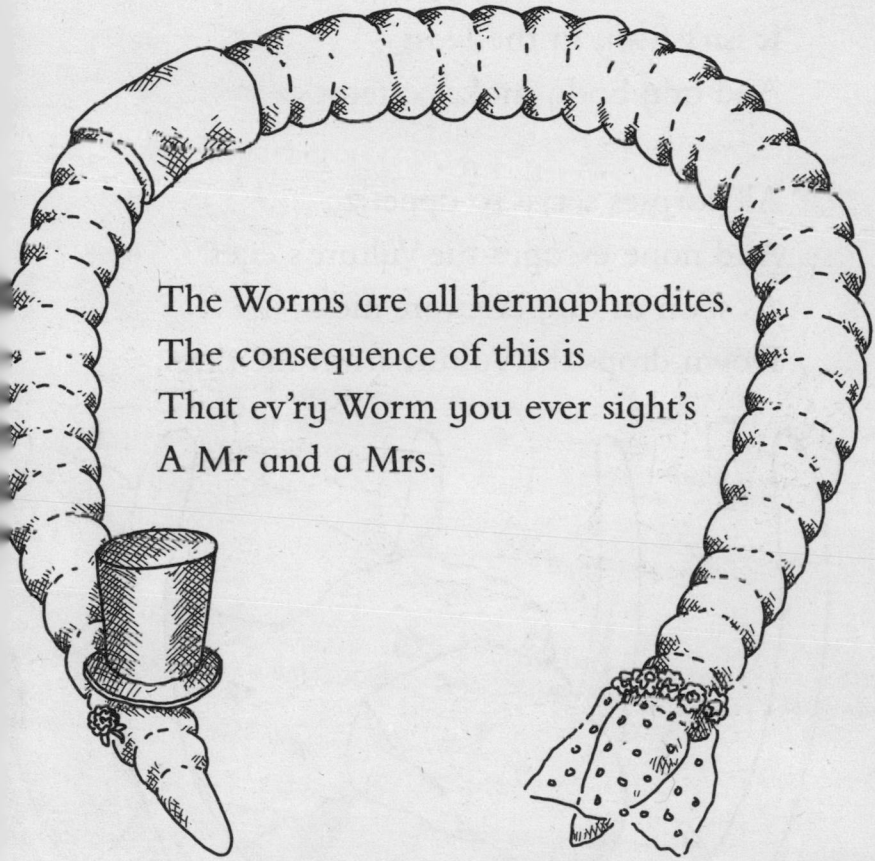

The Worms are all hermaphrodites.
The consequence of this is
That ev'ry Worm you ever sight's
A Mr and a Mrs.

Take Cover

The Vulture feeds on the deceased
Of absolutely ev'ry beast.
It isn't fussy in the least
And any body makes a feast.

All corpses serve to appetize
And none escapes the Vulture's eyes.
As soon as any creature dies,
Down drops the Vulture from the skies.

Remember then – before you're dead –
It's better if you die in bed
Or even in the garden shed
If there are Vultures overhead.

We Have Lift-Off

Young Gannets like practising flying
In their nests on the high narrow ledges.
The impetuous things
Keep on flapping their wings
While perched on the ultimate edges.

But all of the time that they're trying,
They are fearful of premature motion.
So they're careful to stand
Facing in towards land
And keeping their backs to the ocean.

Best Foot Forward

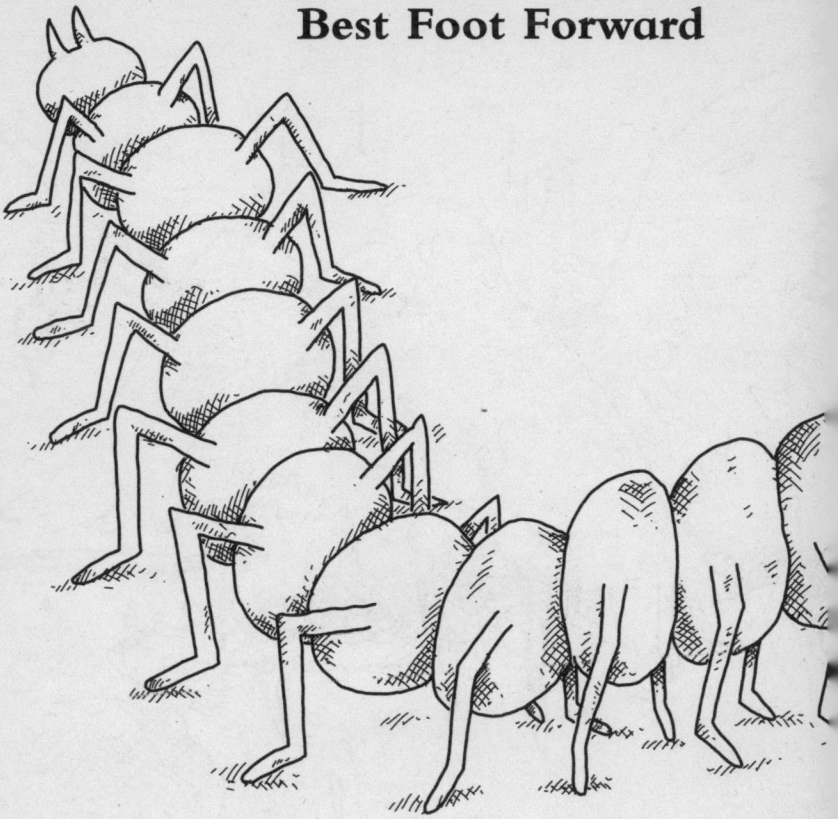

You thought the Centipede possessed
Exactly fifty pairs of feet?
Is that the figure you'd have guessed?
The answer isn't quite so neat.

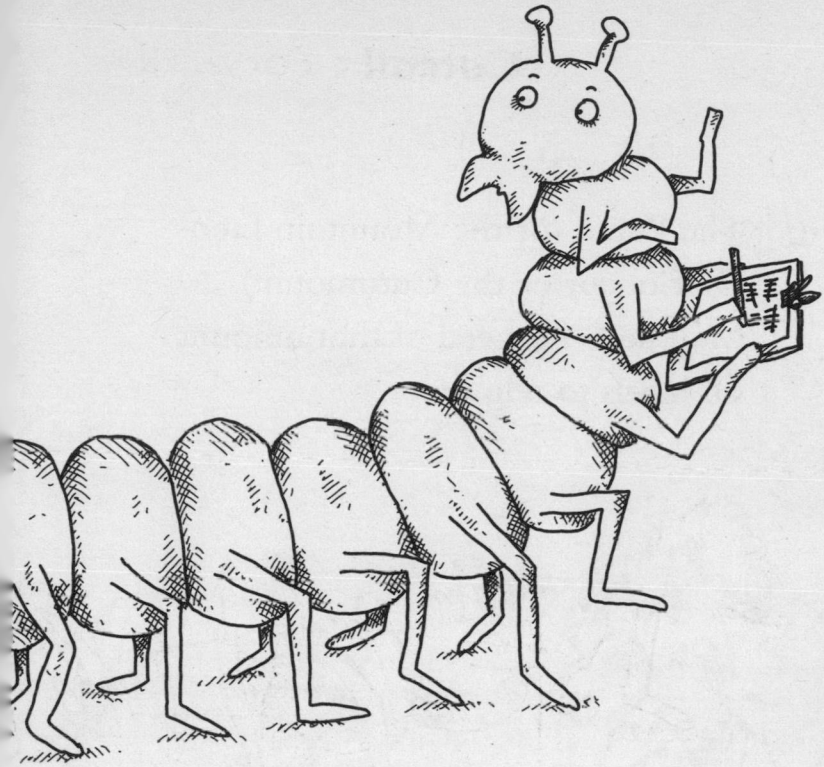

For scientific men who've seen
Each centipedal cousin,
Find some have only got fifteen
And some have fifteen dozen.

Catcall

The Puma (or the Mountain Lion
Or Cougar or the Catamount)
May have no need of that amount
Of labels to rely on.

But when he fancies lambs to eat
All farmers curse him till they're hoarse.
They call the Puma names too coarse
And vulgar to repeat.

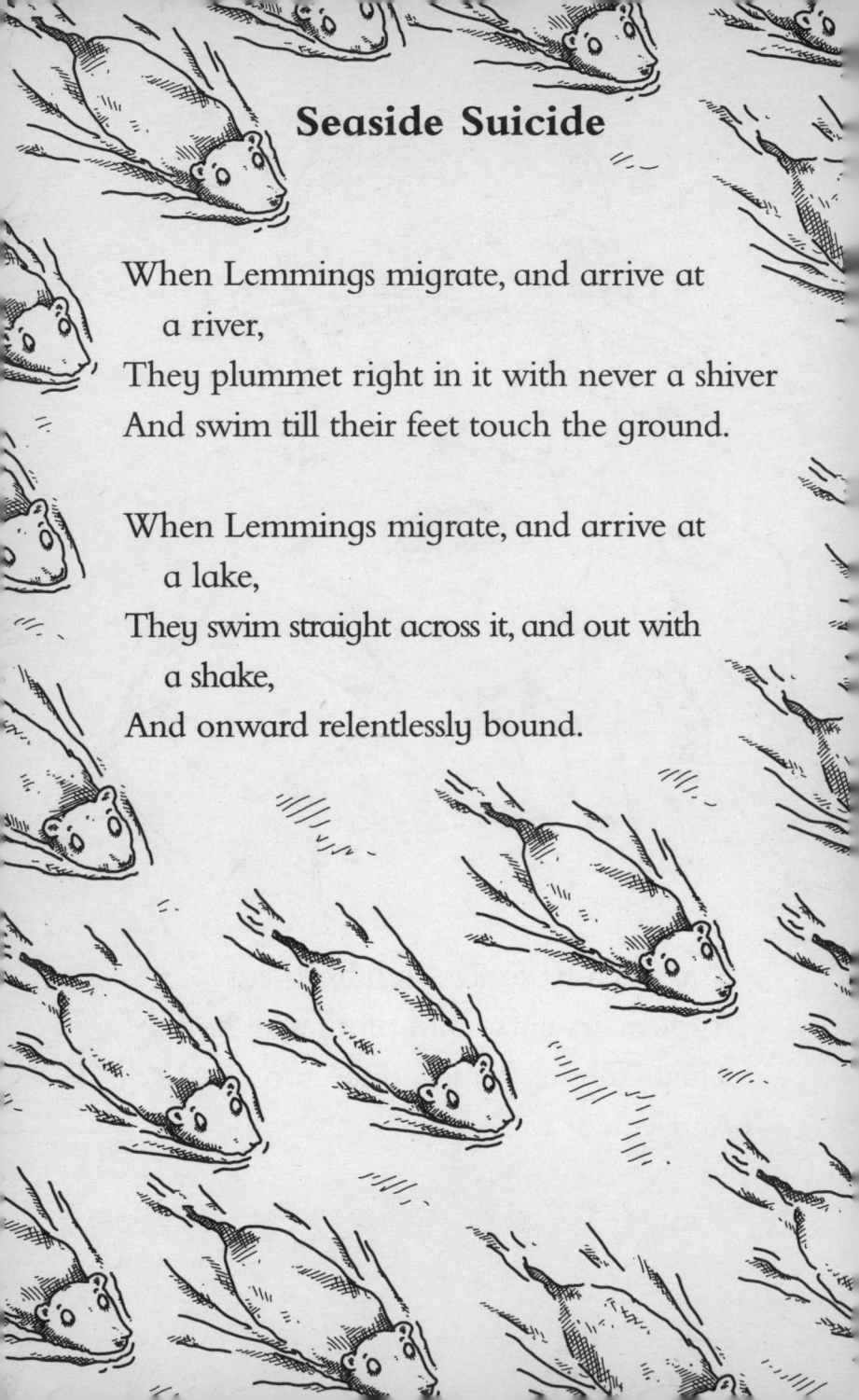

Seaside Suicide

When Lemmings migrate, and arrive at
a river,
They plummet right in it with never a shiver
And swim till their feet touch the ground.

When Lemmings migrate, and arrive at
a lake,
They swim straight across it, and out with
a shake,
And onward relentlessly bound.

And then, when the Lemmings' migratory
host
Has crossed the whole land and arrived at the
coast,
They swim out to sea and are drowned.

Like It or Lump It

The Camel sports a brace of humps,
The Dromedary only one.
It looks as though it's in the dumps
And never having any fun.
The reason, so the experts tell us,
Is that the Dromedary's jealous.

A Family Picnic

If you meet with a man-eating Tiger,
Don't think that it only eats men.
When it's polished off Dad, it'll start on your
mother,
Your sister, your auntie, your new baby
brother,
And shortly be hungry again.

For afters, it might manage you and your gran,
So don't think a man-eater only eats man.

Tale of a Tail

The Boodie is a quarter-size
Relation of the Kangaroo.
You hardly would believe your eyes
When witnessing what Boodies do
To make their nests. Each picks up straw
And puts it on its hairy tail
Which curls around, to squeeze it more
And more, and make a little bale.

Salute the Boodie, tail compactly curled!
First-ever pick-up baler in the world!

Fore and Aft

The Mole, which tunnels very well,
Can find its way by touch and smell:
The many bristles on its nose
Send messages as down it goes.
And though it's practically blind,
It has a sensitive behind –
Just one of Nature's many mercies
And useful when the Mole reverses.

Horse Sense

The Suffolk Punch eats grass for lunch
In spring and summer – that's to say,
In winter it is fed on hay.
There is a difference of course
From any lesser breed of horse –
The Suffolk Punch eats twice as munch.

Free Ride

When the babies of the Crocodile
Hatch out beside the River Nile,
And first emerge upon its sandy shores,
She transports her sons and daughters

To the safety of its waters,
Holding all of them within her mighty jaws.
See how tenderly she holds her little crew!
(But I shouldn't let her try it on with you.)

Hear! Hear!

Though you may feel a little fear
If there's an Earwig in your ear,
There is no cause for utter dread –
It can't get right inside your head.

But on the whole it might be best
To shift the creature, lest it nest.
An ear that's used for Earwig-rearing
Could cause you partial loss of hearing.

Phew!

There's nothing on earth that's ever stunk
As bad as a squirt from an angry Skunk.
There's nothing as foul and nothing as strong –
A squirt from a Skunk is the world's worst pong.

You must leave your house, and you can't return
Till they've fumigated it, while you burn
The furnishings and your clothes as well.
You stand there naked and still you smell.

I'll give you a tip (and this is true):
If an angry Skunk ever squirts on you,
The only thing that's of any use
Is a long cold bath in tomato juice.

Fishing Finger

The Aye-Aye has a finger that's
meticulously planned.
It's quite unlike the other fingers
on the Aye-Aye's hand.
It's long and strong and bony and it's
very very thin,
And when he finds a beetle's hole,
the Aye-Aye sticks it in,

Unbends it and extends it and then
wiggles it about,
And pulls a lot of lovely squashy
beetle-larvae out.
Which only goes to demonstrate
what any Aye-Aye knew –
That all these little lemurs have a
very high I.Q.

A Game of Squash

If there's one thing that's worse than a
Headlouse,
Then it must, I suppose, be a Bedlouse.
But as I've understood lice
(And excepting the Woodlice),
Why, the only good louse is a dead louse.

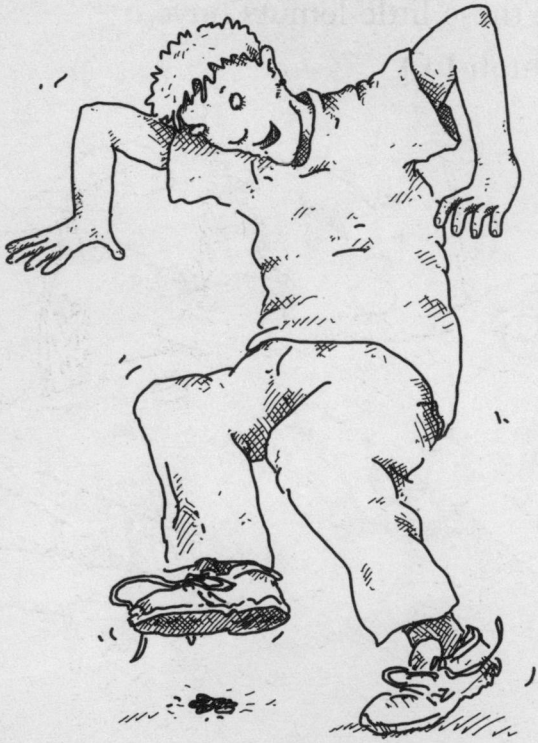

Gulp!

The Pike has one abiding wish –
To swallow any other fish.
It isn't fussy, doesn't mind
What sort, but gobbles any kind.
In fact, it's guaranteed to like
The chance to eat another Pike.

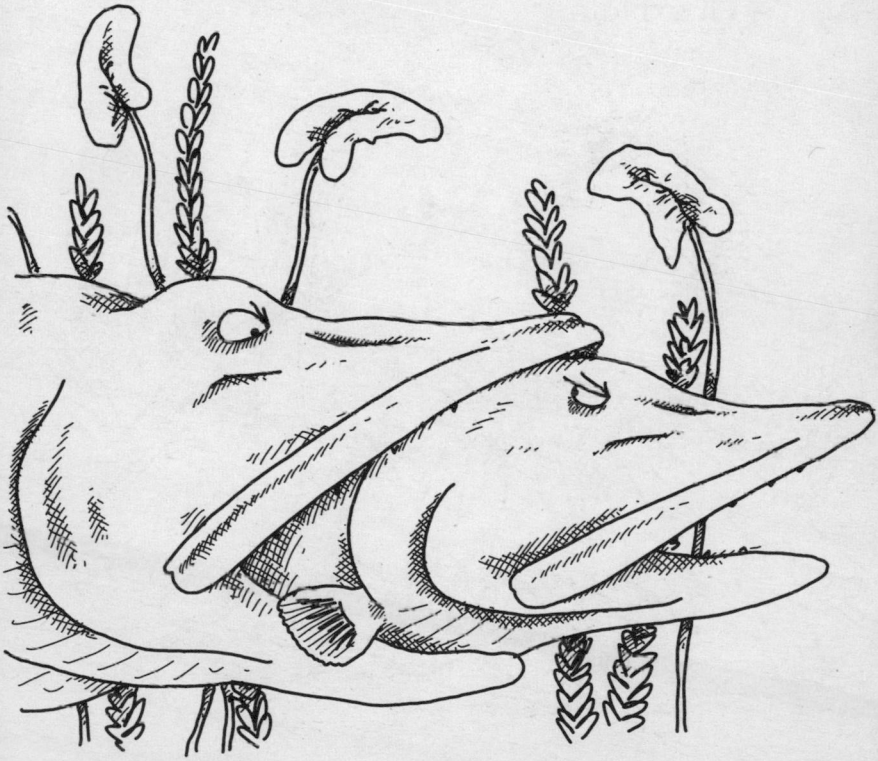

Starting from Scratch

Have you ever been bird-spotting
And observed a Starling squatting
On an ants' nest, and you wonder
As you watch it, why in thunder
Is the silly creature doing
Something it must soon be rueing?
I'll explain.

Parasites that drive it frantic
Make the bird perform this antic,
Knowing ants will then infest it
And efficiently divest it
Of the pests, with formic acid,
Rendering the Starling placid
Once again.

Jolly Blue Giant

The Blue's the biggest kind of Whale
At thirty metres, top to tail.
The largest creature on the earth
(It's seven metres long at birth!)
And as for weight, it's twenty-five
Times any elephant alive.
If you should meet one face to face,
You need not swim away apace
In fear, or even show alarm,
The Blue won't do you any harm.
It isn't that Blue Whales are wimps.
It's just that all they eat is shrimps.

Down the Hatch

The Python can unlock its jaws
To gape as wide as double doors,
And then the snake expands its throat
And swallows whole a nanny-goat
Or pig or antelope or sheep,
And goes contentedly to sleep,

Its middle one enormous bulge,
The shape of which does not divulge
What wretched animal has died.
Let's hope it's never you inside
The Python. If it were, my friend,
That, without doubt, would be

THE END

ABOUT THE AUTHOR

Dick King-Smith was born in 1922 in Bitton, Gloucestershire. He is father, grandfather and great-grandfather to his ever-extending family and he likes nothing better than to surround himself with them.

Dick was a soldier, serving as a Lieutenant in the Grenadier Guards during World War II from 1941-1946. He then enjoyed a twenty-year career as a farmer, going on to try his luck at being a salesman, a factory worker and eventually a primary-school teacher, before hitting on the one thing he truly loved to do – tell stories. Dick now devotes his time to writing and has become one of the top ten best-selling children's authors in the UK.

All kinds of animals have played important roles in Dick King-Smith's life, especially pigs, for which he has a great fondness. His book *The Sheep-Pig* won the Guardian Award in 1984, and was later made into the irresistible motion picture, *Babe.*

When asked what he likes best about being a children's author, Dick replies, "Getting thousands of letters from children (and adults) all over the world, saying they've enjoyed what I do."

Dick's favourite place is his seventeenth-century cottage near Bristol – located only three miles from his birthplace. He writes all of his books in a small study, from where he's able to look out of the window at the countryside and retreat into his special world of fantasy, skilfully placing words into the mouths of the animal characters that he knows and loves so well.

Also available by Dick King-Smith, award-winning author and creator of BABE:

From Corgi Books, for older readers
GODHANGER
THE CROWSTARVER

From Corgi Yearling Books
MR APE
A MOUSE CALLED WOLF
HARRIET'S HARE

From Young Corgi/Doubleday Books
ALL BECAUSE OF JACKSON
BILLY THE BIRD
CONNIE AND ROLLO
E.S.P.
FUNNY FRANK
THE GUARD DOG
HORSE PIE
OMNIBOMBULATOR

From Corgi Pups, for beginner readers
HAPPY MOUSEDAY

From Corgi (Poetry)
DIRTY GERTIE MACKINTOSH

And coming soon from Doubleday Books ...
TITUS RULES OK!

Also available by Jonathan Allen:

From Picture Corgi Books

CHICKEN LICKEN
THE UGLY DUCKLING

And coming soon from Picture Corgi Books …
LITTLE RED HEN

BILLY THE BIRD

Dick King-Smith

"Look at me, I'm flying!"

Mary's little brother Billy seems perfectly normal, until one moonlit evening Mary finds him floating above his bed, with his nose, tummy and toes touching the ceiling. Mary is astounded. Never before has anyone in Mary's family been able to fly – even though their name is Bird!

From then on, whenever the full moon rises, Mary, Lilyleaf (the cat) and Mr Keylock (the guinea pig) stand guard as Billy the Bird flies up, up and away – and home again!

"Dick King-Smith has brought magic into the lives of millions of children' *Parents Magazine*

ISBN 0 552 54678

FUNNY FRANK

Dick King-Smith

"I've got a chicken that wants to be a duck!"

Frank is a funny chick. Unlike all his brothers and sisters, he doesn't want to peck around at anything and everything in the dust. No, Frank wants to dabble about in the lovely duckpond, splashing himself with water. Most of all, he wants to learn to *swim*.

Can Jemima, the farmer's daughter, find a way to help Frank? And if Frank *can* swim like a duck, what will happen when he grows up to be a cockerel?

A hilarious new tale from the master of animal tales, Dick King-Smith, creator of BABE.

'Sparkling humour and wonderful characters are Dick King-Smith's trademarks'
Books for Your Children

0 385 602456

All Transworld titles are available by post from:

Book Service By Post, PO Box 29,
Douglas, Isle of Man, IM99 lBQ

Credit cards accepted.
Please telephone 01624 836000, fax 01624 837003
or Internet http://www.bookpost.co.uk or e-mail:
bookshop@enterprise.net for details

Free postage and packing in the UK.
Overseas customers: allow £1 per book (paperbacks)
and £3 per book (hardbacks).